# THE

# BREXSHIT

## BOOK

FIRST PUBLISHED IN THE UNITED KINGDOM
IN 2016 BY

PORTICO
43 GREAT ORMOND STREET
LONDON
WC1N 3HZ

AN IMPRINT OF THE PAVILION BOOKS COMPANY LTD

ISBN 9781911042693

A CIP CATALOGUE RECORD FOR THIS BOOK IS
AVAILABLE FROM THE BRITISH LIBRARY.

10 9 8 7 6 5

PRINTED AND BOUND BY CPI GROUP (UK) LTD CHATHAM

DESIGNED AND ILLUSTRATED BY BECKY BRICE.

THIS BOOK CAN BE ORDERED DIRECT FROM THE
PUBLISHER AT WWW.PAVILIONBOOKS.COM

# THE

# BREXSHIT

## BOOK

A REMAINER'S SELF-HELP

GUIDE TO LEAVING THE EU

**PORTICO**

# SWITCH OFF

GO BACK IN TIME TO A SIMPLER EXISTENCE, BEFORE BRITAIN JOINED THE EU.

FOR EXAMPLE, SWITCH OFF ALL YOUR DEVICES.

IMAGINE A WORLD WITHOUT TWITTER, TEXTING OR THE INTERNET. BE IN THIS PEACEFUL MOMENT AND TRY TO RELAX.

... BORING, ISN'T IT?

# TACKLING THE FIVE
## STAGES OF GRIEF

### 1. ANGER

PLACE THE PICTURE OF NIGEL FARAGE BELOW OVER
SOMETHING SOFT (E.G. A PILLOW) AND PUNCH IT
REPEATEDLY UNTIL YOU FEEL BETTER.

# BEWARE!!

# UNLEASH YOUR INNER

## COIFFEUR

GIVE BORIS A NEW HAIRCUT TO HELP
HIM IN HIS DYNAMIC NEW
ROLE AT THE FOREIGN OFFICE.

OR JUST DRAW A DUNCE HAT?

# BE CREATIVE

YOU'RE THE DIRECTOR OF THE NEW
MARVEL SUPERHERO MOVIE:

## 'THE BREXITEERS'

WHEN CASTING THERE ARE THREE
MAIN ROLES TO FILL.

SUPER BENDY
BUS BLOKE

X - GOVE

THE NIGEL

WRITE A BRIEF SYNOPSIS OF THE
PLOT BELOW, MAYBE OUR HEROES HAVE
TO CONVINCE THE COUNTRY OF AN
IMPENDING APOCALYPSE, AND HAVE TO
USE ANY MEANS NECESSARY TO ACHIEVE
THEIR GOALS?

WHAT STORIES MIGHT THEY INVENT TO
CONVINCE PEOPLE?

_____

_____

_____

_____

_____

_____

_____

WHO WOULD YOU CAST TO PLAY THE MAIN ROLES?
CHOOSE FROM THE LIST BELOW AND DRAW
A LINE TO THE CHARACTER ON THE PREVIOUS PAGE.

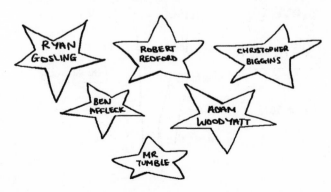

RYAN GOSLING

ROBERT REDFORD

CHRISTOPHER BIGGINS

BEN AFFLECK

ADAM WOODYATT

MR TUMBLE

# BREXIT WORDSEARCH

| A | R | S | P | O | J | E | R | E | M | Y |
|---|---|---|---|---|---|---|---|---|---|---|
| Z | U | G | B | X | A | D | W | B | T | E |
| C | I | F | A | I | L | U | R | E | V | J |
| L | N | Y | N | L | Y | N | C | O | L | O |
| R | E | B | A | H | T | C | G | K | I | H |
| M | D | Z | N | V | S | A | O | U | A | N |
| O | G | S | A | I | J | N | F | D | R | S |
| V | V | S | X | M | G | P | H | M | S | O |
| U | B | E | W | C | R | E | L | A | X | N |
| D | F | A | R | A | G | E | L | Y | S | I |

| GOVE | FAILURE | LIARS |
|------|---------|-------|
| OVER | BANANA | NHS |
| RELAX | RUINED | JEREMY |
| JOHNSON | MAY | NIGEL |
| FARAGE | DUNCAN | |

# ANGER CHUNNEL

IGNITE YOUR EMOTIONS & RATIONALISE YOUR FEELINGS. HOW DOES THIS IMAGE MAKE YOU FEEL?

# DEEPEST SECRET FEARS

TAKE A MOMENT AND DIVE INTO
    YOUR MIND POOL.

ANSWER THESE QUESTIONS AS HONESTLY
AS YOU CAN, AND THEN SIT WITH
THEM AND COME TO TERMS WITH
    WHAT THEY COULD MEAN.

1  WHAT IS YOUR DEEPEST
   SECRET FEAR?

   _____

   _____

   _____


2  WHAT DO YOU THINK IS THE
   BEST WAY FOR YOU TO COME
   TO TERMS WITH THIS FEAR?

   _____

   _____

   _____

EVERYBODY HAS FEARS. HERE ARE SOME
IMAGINED ANSWERS FROM PEOPLE IN
THE PUBLIC EYE TO HELP YOU.

## NIGEL FARAGE

FEAR: PEOPLE LAUGHING AT ME

RESOLVE: GLOATING!!! WHO'S LAUGHING NOW?
HA, HA, HA. HA. HA. I'M LAUGHING NOW!

## BORIS JOHNSON

FEAR: DEALING WITH THE CONSEQUENCES
OF MY ACTIONS.

RESOLVE: NOT TO WORRY, ALL THE CHAPS
FROM THE CLUB WILL HELP ME OUT
SHOULD I GET IN THE SOUP AGAIN.
DAVE CAN PULL A FEW STRINGS!

## JEREMY CORBYN

FEAR: POTATOES

RESOLVE: OVER THE YEARS I HAVE DEVELOPED
A DELICIOUS RECIPE FOR A ROOT VEGETABLE
STEW UTILISING CARROTS, SWEDES,
TURNIPS, BUT NO POTATOES!

# THOUGHT PAD

IMAGINE THE RESULTS OF THE
REFERENDUM ARE NOT YET IN.
USE THIS PAGE TO DRAW
YOUR OWN CONCLUSIONS.

DRAW HERE.

# ASK JEREMY

## SELF-LOATHING

"DEAR JEREMY - I CAN'T HELP
THINKING THAT EVERYONE HATES ME.
I PUT ON A FACADE OF BONHOMIE
& PRETEND I'M EVERYONE'S BEST MATE
BUT WHEN I GO HOME I CRY WITH
MY TEDDY...
ALSO I HAVE HYGIENE ISSUES."
         NIGEL (KENT)

JEREMY SAYS:

WOW. YOU HAVE HAD A
TOUGH TIME. NOT SURE I
CAN HELP. HAVE YOU
TRIED YOGA?

# PR GURU

USE THIS PAGE TO DESIGN A REMAIN
POSTER THAT MIGHT ACTUALLY
MAKE A DIFFERENCE & NOT
BE INSTANTLY FORGETTABLE

YOUR SLOGAN HERE:

# PHILOSOPHY SOFA

DID DAVID CAMERON ACTUALLY

EVER EXIST?

DISCUSS...

# BRAIN SPRINT

WHERE'S GOVE HIDING?

ANSWER: HE'S HIDING UNDER THE SLIDE BECAUSE HE'S MADE A TERRIBLE MESS AND HE'S LET HIMSELF DOWN.

# IMAGINEERING

USING YOUR IMAGINATION CAN HELP YOU
DE-STRESS AND RE-FOCUS. READ THROUGH
THE BEGINNING OF THE STORY AND THEN
FINISH IT OFF ON THE NEXT PAGE.


ONCE UPON A TIME THERE WERE FOUR
BROTHERS. THE OLDEST BROTHER DAVID
HAD RULED THE LAND HAPPILY GOING
ABOUT DOING WHATEVER HE PLEASED,
BUT THE BROTHERS BORIS, NIGEL AND
MICHAEL WERE JEALOUS. AT NIGHT
THEY EACH WENT OFF TO THEIR
CHAMBERS AND PLOTTED AND PLANNED
AND PLOTTED AND PLANNED.
THEN BORIS HAD AN IDEA! WHAT
IF THEY GOT TOGETHER AND
INVENTED AN EVIL MONSTER THAT
THEY COULD PERSUADE THE PEOPLE
WAS OUT TO DESTROY EVERYBODY...

FINISH THE STORY BELOW.

SEE IF YOU CAN IMAGINE WHAT
MIGHT HAPPEN? WOULD THE PEOPLE
BELIEVE SUCH LUDICROUS AND
RIDICULOUS LIES?

_____
_____
_____
_____
_____
_____
_____
_____
_____
_____
_____

*The End*

# BREXIT BLANKET

- LOOK OUT THE WINDOW

- CAN YOU SEE YOUR CLOSE NEIGHBOURS?

- DO THEY SEEM HAPPY?

- ARE THEY SAFE?

- ARE THEY PROSPEROUS?

- DO THEY SEEM TO WANT TO SHARE

    THEIR HAPPINESS, SECURITY
    AND PROSPERITY WITH YOU?


IF SO, WHY NOT NAIL A HEAVY BLANKET
OVER THE WINDOW SO YOU CAN
    PRETEND THEY'RE NOT THERE?

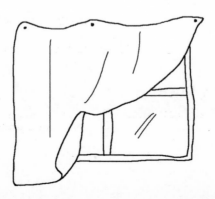

I WAS RIGHT,
YOU WERE WRONG

I WAS RIGHT,
YOU WERE WRONG

I WAS RIGHT,
YOU WERE WRONG

I WAS RIGHT,
YOU WERE WRONG.

I WAS RIGHT,
YOU WERE WRONG

MANTRA

I WAS RIGHT,
YOU WERE WRONG

I WAS RIGHT,
YOU WERE WRONG

I WAS RIGHT,
YOU WERE WRONG

I WAS RIGHT,
YOU WERE WRONG

I WAS RIGHT,
YOU WERE WRONG

I WAS RIGHT,
YOU WERE WRONG

# LEARN TO LAUGH AGAIN

LAUGHING CAN BE THE GREATEST HEALER.

HAVE A CHUCKLE AT THIS LIMERICK:

"THERE WAS A YOUNG FELLOW FROM HOVE,

WHO COULDN'T ABIDE MICHAEL GOVE,

AFTER BREXIT HE WROTE,

A SHORT SUICIDE NOTE,

AND OFF BRIGHTON PIER HE DOVE!"

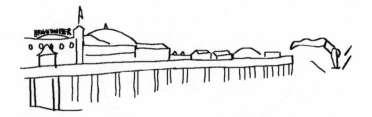

# NEGATIVITY SALAD

## INGREDIENTS:

- 1 x CUPFUL OF FINANCIAL INSTABILITY
- 2 x TABLESPOONS OF WEAKENED NATIONAL SECURITY
- A BUNCH OF CASUAL RACISM
- 500G OF CRUSHED DREAMS

MIX THEM ALL IN A BIG SALAD BOWL AND GARNISH WITH YOUR OWN TEARS.

YOU NOW HAVE 2 CHOICES:

- EAT IT AND LET IT ROT YOU FROM INSIDE

OR

- LIGHTLY TOSS IT OUT THE WINDOW

# HURDLES TO HAPPINESS

IMAGINE YOU'RE RUNNING A RACE.
ON THE TRACK IN FRONT OF YOU ARE ALL
THE HURDLES YOU'LL NEED TO OVERCOME
IF YOU ARE GOING TO BE HAPPY IN A
POST-BREXIT WORLD.

THE STARTER PISTOL FIRES.

- JUMP OVER THE HURDLE OF REGRET

- LEAP OVER THE HURDLE OF DISAPPOINTMENT

- SOAR OVER THE HURDLE OF BROKEN DREAMS

- SMASH FULL PELT INTO THE HURDLE OF YOUR
  SMUG BREXIT-VOTING FRIEND/RELATIVE/
  MORTGAGE ADVISOR AND COMPLETELY
  OBLITERATE IT.

FEELING HAPPIER?

# BROADEN YOUR HORIZONS

LEARN A NEW LANGUAGE!

TRANSLATE THIS FRENCH SENTENCE:

PAS TOUS D'ENTRE NOUS ONT VOTÉ
À QUITTER, ET IL EST VRAIMENT
OK POUR MOI DE QUITTER MES
CHIENS POOP LE TROTTOIR? *

* NOT ALL OF US VOTED TO LEAVE,
   AND IS IT REALLY OK FOR ME TO
LEAVE MY DOG'S POOP ON THE PAVEMENT?

# MEDITATION

IMAGINE YOURSELF ON AN ISLAND,
COMPLETELY CUT OFF FROM CIVILISATION...

CONGRATULATIONS, YOU'RE
HALF WAY THERE TO ACCEPTANCE.

# CORBYN CRAFT CORNER:

## WOOD WORK

HAVING TROUBLE PUTTING TOGETHER YOUR OWN SHADOW CABINET?

NEVER MIND, WHY NOT FASHION YOUR OWN ACTUAL **REAL** CABINET OUT OF SOME LOVELY OAK?

AND GET SOME QUALITY ME TIME TO BOOT!

# BE INDEPENDENT

GIVE YOURSELF THE SPACE
TO FORGET ABOUT BREXIT BLUES

MOVE TO SCOTLAND, MARRY A SCOT
& AWAIT YOUR EU PASSPORT ON INDEPENDENCE.

# EMBRACE CHANGE
## POST REFERENDUM

REPLACEMENTS FOR A EUROPEAN DIET:

OLIVE OIL → LARD

PIZZA → CHEESE ON TOAST

PAELLA → RICE PUDDING

OLIVES → PICKLED EGGS

# FORGIVENESS FLUTE

WHY NOT USE THE KEYS ON THIS FLUTE
OF FORGIVENESS TO NAME WHO YOU
BLAME FOR YOUR NEGATIVE FEELINGS.
DON'T FORGET TO INCLUDE YOURSELF!

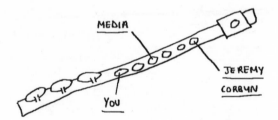

NOW SOFTLY PLAY THE FLUTE &
BLOW THE NEGATIVITY AWAY.

# EXPLORE YOUR MOMENT

IMAGINE YOU'RE HOLDING 28 SHINY
YELLOW BALLOONS.

LET 27 OF THEM FLY AWAY.
YOU ARE LEFT HOLDING THE ONE
SLOWLY DEFLATING BALLOON.

OH NO... IT BURST

# LEARN TO SAY GOODBYE

DEAR LATVIA,

I JUST WANTED TO REACH OUT TO YOU AND SHARE MY FEELINGS WITH YOU. ALTHOUGH WE HAVE BEEN PARTNERS FOR THE LAST 12 YEARS I REALLY DON'T FEEL THAT I HAVE GOT TO KNOW YOU AT ALL? IT SEEMS WHAT WITH ONE THING AND ANOTHER IT IS ALL OVER BEFORE IT REALLY BEGAN! ANYHOO, I JUST WANTED TO WISH YOU ALL THE BEST AND SAY THAT YOU ARE MORE THAN WELCOME TO COME VISIT ANY TIME YOU LIKE (ASSUMING YOU HAVE THE CORRECT PAPERWORK AND DON'T EXPECT TO EARN ANY MONEY WHILE YOU ARE VISITING).

LOVE GB x

# BLUE - SKY THINKING

YOU MIGHT HAVE LOST THE REFERENDUM
BUT AT LEAST YOU'VE GAINED A FRIEND.

# DE-STRESS POST BREXIT

PLAN A REWARDING EVENING OUT FOR YOU
AND YOUR PARTNER.

GO FOR A DELICIOUS ~~ITALIAN~~ FISH & CHIPS
SUPPER, WASHED DOWN WITH A LARGE
GLASS OF ~~CHIANTI~~ BOVRIL. THEN
ON TO THE ~~OPERA~~ SWIMMING BATHS,
TOPPING OFF THE EVENING WITH
A ROMANTIC STROLL DOWN THE
~~BOULEVARD~~ PRECINCT.

# POSITIVE SPIN

B RAVE
R EQUISITE
E XCITING
X YLOPHONE
I NCLUSIVE
T HOUGHTFUL

# A'MAZE'ING YOU

TRY TO MAKE YOUR WAY THROUGH THE MAZE, AVOIDING BREXIT PITFALLS AS YOU GO.

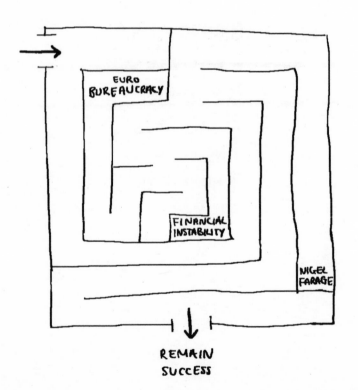

# THIS IS NOT

# A DREAM

# REWARD STATION

DID YOU CURSE YOURSELF
TODAY FOR BELIEVING YOUR
FACEBOOK FEED WHEN IT
SUGGESTED A LANDSLIDE
VICTORY FOR REMAIN?
YOU DIDN'T? GREAT. HAVE
A WEETABIX.

# BREXIT PETTING ZOO

LEARN TO LOVE YOUR ADVERSARY.
PERSONALISE THEM.

STROKE YOUR
DAVID CAMERON
KITTEN.

# TACKLING THE FIVE STAGES OF GRIEF.

## 2. DENIAL

FACE YOUR GRIEF.
THERE WILL NOT BE ANOTHER
REFERENDUM, NO MATTER HOW
DRUNK YOU GET.

# POKÉMON GOVE

USING YOUR POKÉMON GOVE BALL,
HEAD OUT ON THE STREETS AND
SEE IF YOU CAN FIND AND
CAPTURE MICHAEL GOVE.

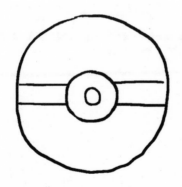

GOTTA CATCH HIM ALL!

# STOP

# WEEPING

# BUTTON BONANZA

HOW MANY BUTTONS CAN YOU
THINK OF TO REPLACE ARTICLE 50 WITH?

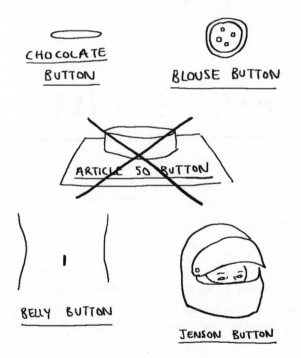

CHOCOLATE
BUTTON

BLOUSE BUTTON

ARTICLE 50 BUTTON

BELLY BUTTON

JENSON BUTTON

# RECOGNISE YOUR ACHIEVEMENTS

REWARD YOURSELF FOR GOOD WORK.
MAKE A LIST OF SOME OF YOUR GOALS
AND SOME REWARDS FOR COMPLETING THEM.

## SOME EXAMPLES:

| GOALS | REWARDS |
|---|---|
| • FINISH YOUR TAX RETURN A WEEK BEFORE THE DEADLINE. | • A NICE GLASS OF CHILLED PROSECCO. |
| • THROW OUT ALL THE OLD CLOTHES YOU DON'T NEED ANY MORE AND DECLUTTER. | • GO TO THE CINEMA WITH A FRIEND. |
| • LEAD YOUR COUNTRY INTO ECONOMIC AND CULTURAL UNCERTAINTY BY ANNOUNCING AN UNNECESSARY EU REFERENDUM. | • A LIFE PEERAGE AND INTERNATIONAL LECTURE TOUR NETTING UP TO £400K PER TALK. |

NOW DO YOUR OWN HERE
↓

| GOALS | REWARDS |
|-------|---------|
| • | • |
| • | • |
| • | • |

# MORE REASONS TO BE CHEERFUL:

- WH SMITH
- BARRY SHEENE
- SOUTHEND ADVENTURE ISLAND
- MORPH
- RICHARD STILGOE
- JELLIED EELS
- NATIONAL EXPRESS
- COUNTRYFILE
- KENDAL MINT CAKE
- IMPENETRABLE DIALECTS

# BE CREATIVE

IMAGINE THE ALTERNATIVE RESULT TO THE REFERENDUM.

NOW IMAGINE THE NEWSPAPER HEADLINES.

WRITE THEM DOWN.

NOW BATHE IN THAT GLORY & RETAIN THAT FEELING FOR AS LONG AS YOU CAN.

# SOOTHE YOURSELF

COLOUR IN THIS BEAUTIFUL
FLOWER THAT HAS 28 PETALS.

WHOOPS, ONE'S FALLEN OFF...

# ANGER CHUNNEL

IGNITE YOUR EMOTIONS & RATIONALISE YOUR FEELINGS. HOW DOES THIS IMAGE MAKE YOU FEEL?

# PHOTOSYNTHESIS

ON THE LEFT BELOW STICK A
PHOTO OF YOURSELF BEFORE BREXIT.

NOW TAKE ANOTHER PHOTO OF
YOURSELF AS YOU ARE NOW AND
PASTE THIS ON THE RIGHT.

NOTICE ANYTHING DIFFERENT? NO?
THAT'S BECAUSE - APART FROM BEING
SIGNIFICANTLY WORSE OFF, MUCH MORE
LIKELY TO LOSE YOUR JOB AND
GENERALLY FACING AN UNCERTAIN
FUTURE - YOU'RE STILL
THE SAME PERSON

# NEW RELATIONSHIPS

WHEN RELATIONSHIPS END, IT'S EASY TO MOURN WHAT YOU'VE LOST.

BUT THE GOOD THING IS THAT NOW YOU'RE FREE TO START NEW RELATIONSHIPS WITH ANYONE YOU LIKE.

HOW ABOUT A HUNKY, RICH RUSSIAN OLIGARCH?

OR A YOUNG, FREE - SPIRITED THINKER?

OR HOW ABOUT A DELUSIONAL BUSINESS TYCOON WITH A BACKCOMBED SHIH-TZU ON HIS HEAD?

# RE - APPROPRIATION

HOW MANY USES CAN YOU FIND
FOR THE FLAG OF EUROPE?

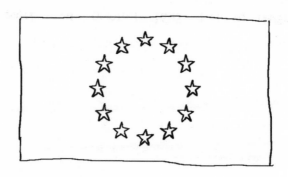

HERE ARE SOME TO GET YOU STARTED:

1. TEA TOWEL

2. BATH MAT

3. ADULT NAPPY

4. HEADSCARF

5. RUCKSACK

6. PAPOOSE

7. BABY CHANGING MAT

8. GROCERY BAG

9. PILLOW CASE

10. TOILET CLOTH

# ASK JEREMY

## LONELINESS

"DEAR JEREMY - I HAVE BEEN VERY
MEAN TO MY BEST FRIEND, AND NOW
HE AND ALL <u>HIS</u> FRIENDS WON'T
TALK TO ME. I HAVE SO MUCH LOVE
TO GIVE, BUT NO ONE TO GIVE IT
TO. I AM SO LONELY."
MICHAEL (SURREY)

<u>JEREMY SAYS</u>:
DEAR OH DEAR OH DEAR...
HMM, WHAT TO DO?
ANYHOO, MUST DASH.

# SCREAM INTO YOUR
# PROFANITY PILLOW

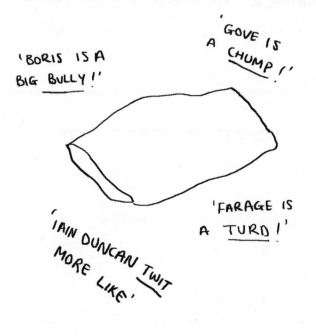

'BORIS IS A BIG BULLY!'

'GOVE IS A CHUMP!'

'FARAGE IS A TURD!'

'IAIN DUNCAN TWIT MORE LIKE!'

# BRAIN SPRINT

## WHERE'S DAVID?

WHATEVER HAPPENED TO OUR ONCE PROUD PM? CAN YOU SPOT HIM?

# AVOID THE 'BLAME GAME'

BLAMING OTHERS IS POINTLESS.

HOWEVER, IT FEELS GOOD SO USE THIS
PAGE TO WRITE DOWN THE NAMES OF
FRIENDS & FAMILY WHO YOU SUSPECT
OF VOTING LEAVE.

# BROADEN YOUR HORIZONS

LEARN A NEW LANGUAGE!

TRANSLATE THIS DUTCH SENTENCE:

IK HOOP BREXIT WON'T DESTABILISEREN
JE ECONOMIE TE VEEL EN NEEM
DAN KAN IK HEB 5 GRAM VAN
HET NORTHERN LIGHT AUB *

* I DO HOPE BREXIT DOESNT DESTABILISE
YOUR ECONOMY TOO MUCH AND
PLEASE MAY I HAVE 5 GRAMMES
OF THE NORTHERN LIGHTS PLEASE.

# CORBYN CRAFT CORNER:

## KNITTING

KNIT A THICK, WOOLLY BALACLAVA.

PUT IT ON.

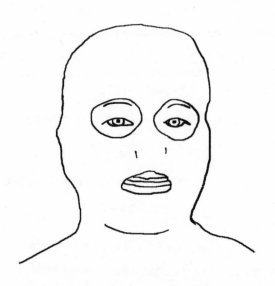

NOW YOU CAN'T HEAR THE

VOICES OF DISSENT.

# MEDITATION ON THE MOVE

INSTEAD OF SITTING AT HOME,
STEWING OVER THE REFERENDUM RESULT,
CLEAR YOUR HEAD BY GOING FOR A
NICE, LONG DRIVE.

BASK IN THE KNOWLEDGE THAT YOU'RE
DRIVING ON THE LEFT-HAND SIDE OF
THE ROAD AND GIVING WAY TO THE
RIGHT AT ROUNDABOUTS,
EXACTLY AS NATURE INTENDED.

STOP OFF AT A WILD BEAN CAFÉ
TO CELEBRATE.

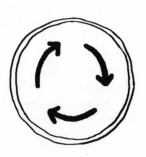

# EMBRACE CHANGE POST

## REFERENDUM

ALTERNATIVES TO EUROPEAN CULTURE:

LA DOLCE VITA → CARRY ON AT YOUR CONVENIENCE

PICASSO → TONY HART

HANS CHRISTIAN ANDERSEN → KATIE PRICE

MOZART → STEPS

MARCEL MARCEAU → LOUIE SPENCE

# DARE TO SOAR

BUT BE CAREFUL NOT TO BURN YOUR WINGS.

# LET IT GO

UNLEASH YOUR INNER RAGE

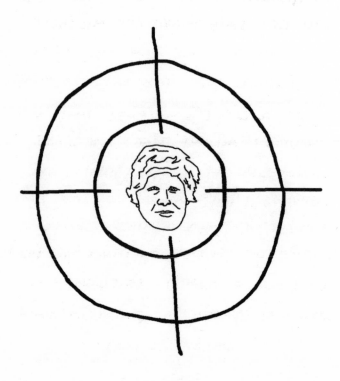

# LEARN TO SAY GOODBYE

DEAR GERMANY,

I THOUGHT IT MIGHT BE A GOOD TIME
TO GET SOME THINGS OFF MY CHEST.
ALTHOUGH WE HAVE WORKED TOGETHER
VERY WELL OVER THE PAST 23 YEARS,
I AM A LITTLE CONCERNED THAT YOU
HAVEN'T ALWAYS HAD MY BEST
INTERESTS AT HEART. NOW I AM
LEAVING I JUST WANTED TO SAY THAT
PERHAPS WE COULD CONSIDER TAKING A
COURSE OF THERAPY TOGETHER TO HELP
US BUILD A ROBUST FRIENDSHIP? IT
WOULD BE TERRIBLE IF WE FELL OUT AGAIN.

ANYWAY, BIG HUGS,

GB x

# GRIEF BALLS

STRUGGLING TO COME TO TERMS WITH
THE REFERENDUM RESULT?

IMAGINE YOUR STAGES OF GRIEF AS
SOCCER FOOTBALLS.

... NOW KICK YOUR FOOTBALLS
INTO THE SOCCER GOAL.

# FOOD THERAPY

TAKE YOUR MIND OFF BREXIT BLUES BY
PREPARING A DELICIOUS SWEET TREAT.

* 300g OF WITNEY STRAWBERRIES
* 300ml OF WHIPPED TATTON
  DOUBLE CREAM
* 4 PRE-PREPARED MERINGUE NESTS
  (MADE FROM FINEST UXBRIDGE EGGS)

MIX IT ALL TOGETHER AND YOU'VE
MADE A RIGHT OLD ETON MESS.

# IMPROVE WELLNESS

STAND UP STRAIGHT WITH A BOOK
ON YOUR HEAD. IMAGINE YOU ARE
HELD UP BY AN IRON ROD, REACHING
HIGH INTO THE CLOUDS.

YOU ARE STRONG.

YOU CAN SUPPORT YOURSELF.

YOU ARE BETTER ALONE.

NO REALLY, YOU ARE
MUCH BETTER ALONE.

CONVINCE YOURSELF
OF THIS.

## POSITIVE SPIN

**G** RACIOUS

**O** PEN

**V** ERY KIND

**E** MPTY

# DISTRACTION ACTIONS

TO STOP YOURSELF WORRYING ABOUT
LEAVING THE EU, TRY SOME OF
THE CLINICALLY PROVEN DISTRACTION
TECHNIQUES LISTED BELOW:

- COUNT UP TO INFINITY IN SEVENS
- HUNT FOR LEGENDARY POKÉMON
- LEARN A NEW LANGUAGE
      (NB - NOT A EUROPEAN ONE)

- WAX ON, WAX OFF

- WORRY ABOUT SOMETHING ELSE
      (ALIEN INVASION, FRACKING ETC.)

# REWARD STATION

DID YOU FANTASISE ABOUT
UNENCUMBERED TRAVEL THROUGH
EUROPE TODAY? IF NOT THEN
WHY NOT REWARD YOURSELF
WITH A JAMMIE DODGER.

# TACKLING THE FIVE STAGES OF GRIEF.

## 3. DEPRESSION

CHEER UP! IT MIGHT NEVER HAPPEN.

OH. WAIT..

# SILVER LININGS

NOW THAT WE'VE LEFT THE EU WE CAN BE JUST LIKE NORWAY, THE FIFTH RICHEST COUNTRY IN THE WORLD.

LIKE NORWAY, WE'LL BE ABLE TO CONTROL OUR OWN AGRICULTURE AND KEEP ALL OUR FISH, RATHER THAN BEING BOUND BY STRICT EU QUOTAS.

ON THE DOWNSIDE, WE'LL ALSO HAVE TO PUT UP WITH MORE TROLLS.

# SEE THINGS FROM THE
## OTHER SIDE

TRY THIS ROLE-PLAY EXERCISE:

- PRETEND YOU'RE AN EXPERT ON HORSES, EVEN THOUGH YOU KNOW NOTHING ABOUT THEM.

- NOW GO TO A BETTING SHOP AND PERSUADE EVERYONE INSIDE TO TAKE A MASSIVE GAMBLE ON THE HORSE THAT'S LEAST LIKELY TO WIN

- WHEN THE HORSE COMES LAST AND EVERYONE HAS LOST THEIR MONEY, QUIETLY LEAVE VIA THE BACK DOOR.

- MAYBE SMOKE A FAG.

NOW YOU'RE THINKING LIKE
NIGEL FARAGE!

# CUT'EM UP COWBOY

WHY NOT TAKE SOME SCISSORS & CUT OUT THE FACES FROM THIS PICTURE OF MICHAEL, BORIS & NIGEL.

PERHAPS IT WILL HELP YOU TO FORGET THEM.

## UNLEASH YOUR INNER

## COIFFEUR

HELP DAVID APPEAR HUMAN.
DRAW ON HIS FAMOUS QUIFF.

# POST-REFERENDUM PAPERCRAFT

## THERAPY

IN THE SQUARE BELOW, DRAW A PICTURE
OF YOUR OWN FACE.

NOW CUT ALONG THE DOTTED LINE
AND OBTAIN A PASSPORT FROM ONE OF
THE 27 REMAINING EU MEMBER
STATES ON THE BLACK MARKET*

CAREFULLY GLUE THE PICTURE OF YOUR
FACE OVER THE PHOTO OF THE PERSON
INSIDE THE PASSPORT.**

CONGRATULATIONS,
YOU'RE BACK IN THE GAME!

* NB, THIS IS ILLEGAL

** NB, THIS IS ALSO ILLEGAL

# CHALLENGE THE BRAIN

SPOT THE DIFFERENCE:

# BE HERE NOW

STAND COMPLETELY STILL, BREATHE
DEEPLY AND CLEAR YOUR MIND.
IT'S HARD BUT TRY TO EMPTY YOUR
HEAD OF ALL THOUGHTS COMPLETELY.

- DON'T THINK ABOUT OTHER PEOPLE

- DON'T THINK ABOUT OTHER PLACES

- DON'T THINK ABOUT ANYTHING
  OR ANYONE AT ALL.

NOW YOU KNOW WHAT IT'S LIKE
TO BE NIGEL FARAGE...

WHERE
YOU'VE
BEEN

WINE

WHISKY

MIDDLE
OF THE
BOOK

BUREAU DE
CHANGE

€ ↑

£ ↓

HALFWAY THROUGH YOUR JOURNEY

WHERE YOU'RE GOING

PASSPORT CONTROL

THIS IS NOT
A REHEARSAL,
GUYS

# BREXIT PETTING ZOO

LEARN TO LOVE YOUR ADVERSARY.
PERSONALISE THEM.

TICKLE PUPPY
BORIS ON HIS
FLUFFY, SOFT
BELLY.

# AROMA   SHAMAN

SMELLS CAN BE POWERFUL EMOTIONAL HEALERS.

THINK OF A SMELL THAT REMINDS

YOU OF THE EU.

IT COULD BE A PARTICULARLY PUNGENT BRIE

YOU ATE IN FRANCE, FOR EXAMPLE,

OR THE BOUQUET OF A PERFECTLY CHILLED

GLASS OF GRÜNER VELTLINER FROM AUSTRIA.

TRY TO RECREATE THE SMELL AND

CAPTURE IT IN THE CIRCLE BELOW—

# ANGER CHUNNEL

IGNITE YOUR EMOTIONS & RATIONALISE YOUR FEELINGS. HOW DOES THIS IMAGE MAKE YOU FEEL?

# SPOT THE DIFFERENCE

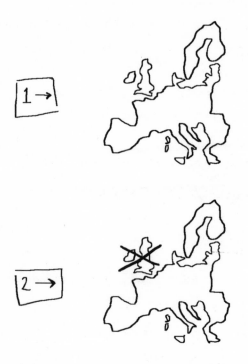

1 →

2 →

ANSWER: IN 2 ITALY IS SLIGHTLY SMALLER

# ASK JEREMY

## BREAK - UPS

"DEAR JEREMY — I HAVE RECENTLY BROKEN OFF A 23-YEAR LONG-TERM RELATIONSHIP, AND I AM NOT SURE I HAVE DONE THE RIGHT THING. I THINK MY SCHOOL CHUMS MIGHT HAVE BULLIED ME INTO MAKING A RASH DECISION. PLEASE HELP."

### DAVID (OXFORDSHIRE)

JEREMY SAYS:

HMM, I CAN SEE THE PROBLEM BUT I AM NOT SURE I CAN COMMIT TO ANSWERING THAT. GOOD LUCK.

# THE GOOD OLD DAYS

IF YOU ARE OLD ENOUGH
TO REMEMBER THE TIME
BEFORE THE EUROPEAN
UNION...

WELCOME BACK
TO THE PAST.

SUNDAY CLOSING

WIDESPREAD INDUSTRIAL ACTION

POWER CUTS

AT LEAST YOU KNOW WHAT
TO EXPECT!

# BROADEN YOUR HORIZONS

LEARN A NEW LANGUAGE!

TRANSLATE THIS | SPANISH | SENTENCE:

LO SIENTO MUCHO DE SER SAUR DE
LA EU, Y PUEDO TENER PARTE
SACRIFICIO DE AQUELLOS ACEITUNAS,
NO, NO LOS QUE CON CHILE
POR FAVOR *

* I AM REALLY SORRY TO BE LEAVING
THE EU AND CAN I HAVE SOME
OF THOSE OLIVES, NO, NOT THE
ONES WITH CHILLI PLEASE.

# AVOIDING THE

## SEPARATION ZONE

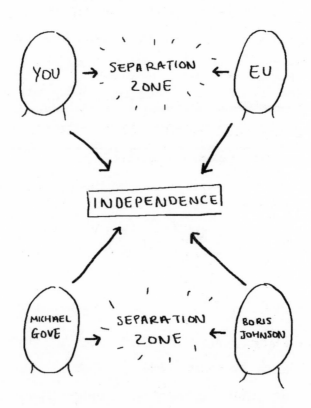

# CORBYN CRAFT CORNER:

## ORIGAMI

TURN ALL THAT NEGATIVITY
INTO SOMETHING BEAUTIFUL.

PICK UP ANY NEWSPAPER
AND, AVOIDING ANY CRITICAL
EDITORIALS ABOUT YOUR ABILITY
TO COMMIT TO THE EU,
FOLD IT INTO AN ORIGAMI SWAN.

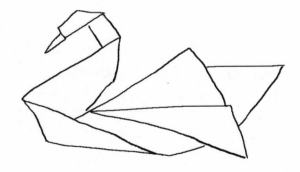

# ORDER YOUR THOUGHTS

- MAKE A LIST OF THE NEGATIVE
  POINTS OF LEAVING THE EU:

_____

_____

_____

_____

_____

_____

_____

_____

_____

_____

_____

- AND NOW MAKE A LIST OF THE
  POSITIVE POINTS OF LEAVING THE EU:

_____

_____

_____

# EMBRACE CHANGE

## POST REFERENDUM

REPLACEMENTS FOR A EUROPEAN DIET #2:

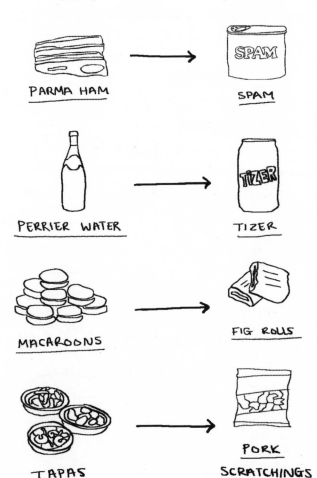

PARMA HAM → SPAM

PERRIER WATER → TIZER

MACAROONS → FIG ROLLS

TAPAS → PORK SCRATCHINGS

# POSITIVITY JAM

TRY TO SEE THE POSITIVE IN
YOUR SITUATION.

FOR EXAMPLE:

HALF EMPTY

BECAUSE WE
LEFT THE EU

HALF FULL

BECAUSE NO ONE
WANTS TO DRINK
ENGLISH WINE.

# LEARN TO SAY GOODBYE

DEAR FRANCE,

BEFORE WE GO OUR SEPARATE WAYS
I JUST WANTED TO CLEAR THE
AIR. I KNOW THAT YOU ARE ANGRY
WITH ME, BUT A CLEAN BREAK IS
SURELY THE BEST WAY TO PROCEED,
AND I HOPE SOMEWHERE DOWN THE
LINE WE CAN BE FRIENDS
REGARDING OUR CD COLLECTION.
I WOULD LIKE ALL THE BEATLES,
BUT YOU CAN KEEP THE
JEAN-MICHEL JARRE!

ALL MY LOVE,
GB X

# POSITIVE SPIN

**B** LAMELESS

**O** BLIGING

**R** ESERVED

**I** NTROVERTED

**S** IMPLE

# MEMORY BOARD

TEST YOUR RECOLLECTION SKILLS AND
SEE IF YOU CAN REMEMBER THESE
PEOPLE AND EVENTS FROM SUMMER 2016...

# REWARD STATION

DID YOU IMAGINE YOURSELF
THROTTLING IAIN DUNCAN SMITH
TODAY? NO? THEN YOU'RE
RECOVERING. REWARD YOURSELF
WITH A CURLY WURLY.

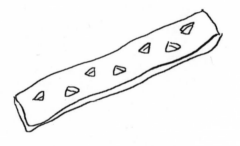

# MAKE A WISH

- CLOSE YOUR EYES AND MAKE A WISH

- NOW OPEN YOUR EYES

IF YOU'RE STILL READING
THIS BOOK, YOUR WISH PROBABLY
HASN'T COME TRUE.

SORRY.

# SILVER LININGS

ALTHOUGH THE POUND IS WORTH A LOT LESS THAN IT WAS, AND WE ARE WELL ON THE WAY TO A RECESSION, AT LEAST YOU WERE RIGHT ALL ALONG!

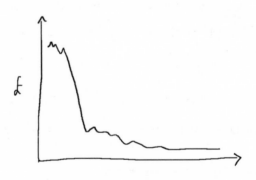

# HOME FROM HOME

MISSING BEING PART OF THE EU?

    THEN WHY NOT RECREATE IT IN

    YOUR OWN HOME?

USE THE FLOORPLAN BELOW TO ASSIGN
EACH MEMBER STATE ITS OWN AREA
OF YOUR HOME.

YOUR KITCHEN COULD BE ITALY, FOR EXAMPLE,
YOUR EN SUITE BATHROOM COULD BE FRANCE,
YOUR AIRING CUPBOARD COULD BE LUXEMBOURG

    AND SO ON...

FOR THE FINISHING TOUCH, VOTE TO LEAVE
YOUR HOUSE AND GO AND LIVE IN YOUR SHED.

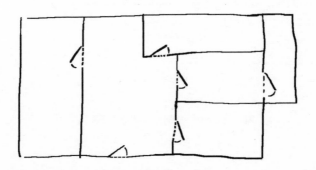

# FOCUS FUNNEL

POUR YOUR DISAPPOINTMENTS INTO THE FUNNEL AND SEE WHAT COMES OUT THE OTHER END...

NB: IT'S NOT ALLOWED TO BE POOP

# TACKLING THE FIVE
## STAGES OF GRIEF.

### 4. BARGAINING

TRY NOT TO FIXATE ON REVERSING THE DECISION.

BIT LATE NOW ANYWAY...

PERHAPS IF CAMERON HAD DONE MORE BARGAINING WITH MERKEL WE WOULDN'T BE IN THIS PICKLE NOW.

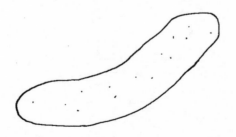

# SWITCH OFF - DE-STRESS

FOLLOW THIS DOT TO DOT AND TRY
NOT TO LET YOUR MIND WANDER ONTO
MORE NEGATIVE ISSUES.

# SEE THINGS FROM THE
## OTHER SIDE

DRAW A BOX LIKE THE ONE BELOW IN
CHALK ON THE PAVEMENT AND STAND IN IT.

IF ANY PASSERS-BY WALK INTO YOUR
BOX PUSH THEM BACK OUT,

EVEN IF THEY'RE TRYING TO
HELP YOU IMPROVE YOUR ECONOMY.

CAN YOU SEE WHY PEOPLE
VOTED LEAVE NOW?

# SPOT THE DIFFERENCE

CHALLENGING YOUR BRAIN CAN HELP
YOU TO BE IN THE MOMENT AND
LIVE WITH YOUR WORRIES. EXAMINE
BOTH IMAGES AND SEE IF YOU CAN
SPOT THE DIFFERENCE.

JEREMY HUNT ENTERING DOWNING
STREET FULLY EXPECTING TO BE
SACKED FROM HIS ROLE AS HEALTH
MINISTER IN THE POST REFERENDUM
CABINET RE-SHUFFLE.

JEREMY HUNT AFTER LEAVING
DOWNING STREET HAVING TO EVERYONE'S
SURPRISE NOT BEEN SACKED FROM HIS
ROLE AS HEALTH MINISTER IN THE POST
REFERENDUM CABINET RE-SHUFFLE.

# EMOTIONAL CACHE

- DO YOU FEEL THE URGE TO SHOUT AT YOUR TV WHENEVER BORIS JOHNSON COMES ON?

- DO YOU WANT TO CRY WHENEVER YOU LOOK AT YOUR SAVINGS ACCOUNT?

- DO YOU HAVE AN IMPULSE TO PUNCH YOUR BREXIT-VOTING FRIEND / FAMILY MEMBER /MORTGAGE ADVISOR WHENEVER HE OR SHE MENTIONS "IMMIGRANTS"?

THESE ARE ALL PERFECTLY NORMAL EMOTIONAL RESPONSES. OR THEY WOULD HAVE BEEN UNDER EU REGULATIONS.

NOW, HOWEVER, YOU'LL NEED TO MANAGE YOUR EMOTIONS THE BRITISH WAY:

BURY THEM IN A <u>DEEP</u> <u>DEEP</u> HOLE AND ONLY LET THEM SURFACE WHEN YOU'RE DRUNK AT CHRISTMAS.

# CONTROL YOUR CONTROL

## URGES

JEREMY IS SITTING ON THE BREXIT FENCE.
HE CAN'T DECIDE WHICH WAY TO FALL.

CAN YOU LEAVE HIM TO IT?
AFTER ALL, IT DOESN'T MATTER
WHAT JEREMY DOES.
JEREMY CAN MAKE HIS OWN MIND UP...
OR CAN HE?

WE ARE
HERE NOW

°0

# BE PROACTIVE

BALLOT PAPER

REMAIN IN EU ☒

LEAVE EU ☐

PHOTOCOPY THIS BALLOT PAPER
1,200,000 TIMES THEN 'DISCOVER'
THEM, THEREBY RENDERING THE
REFERENDUM VOID.

NB, DON'T DO THIS,
IT IS A CRIMINAL ACT.

# BREXIT PETTING ZOO

LEARN TO LOVE YOUR ADVERSARY.
PERSONALISE THEM.

CALM YOUR BRAYING
FARAGE DONKEY.

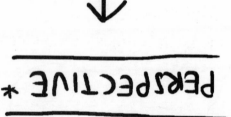

CHANGE YOUR PERSPECTIVE *

\* MOVE TO NEW ZEALAND

# UNLEASH YOUR

# INNER COIFFEUR

HELP MICHAEL CULTIVATE A MORE
MODERN IMAGE. WHAT TYPE
OF BEARD WOULD BE BEST?
DRAW IT ON & COLOUR IT GREY.

REMEMBER...

IT'S NOT

YOUR FAULT.

(UNLESS YOU COULDN'T BE BOTHERED TO VOTE
BECAUSE YOU ASSUMED EVERYONE ELSE
WOULD VOTE REMAIN ANYWAY -
IN WHICH CASE IT IS YOUR FAULT)

# SWITCH OFF AND DE-STRESS

PAINT BY NUMBERS. CALM YOURSELF BY FOLLOWING THE COLOUR CODE TO COMPLETE THIS MAP.

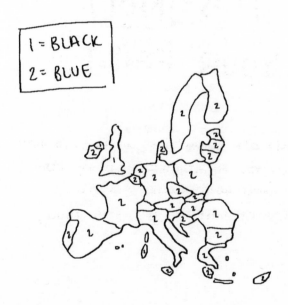

# EVEN MORE REASONS TO

## BE CHEERFUL:

- BULLSEYE
- RICHARD MADELEY
- CONCORD
- SALLY GUNNELL
- THE WURZELS
- BBC RADIO 3
- BASINGSTOKE
- SUET PUDDING
- SWAN VESTAS
- COUNCIL ESTATES

# GROW YOUR OWN RECOVERY

POST BREXIT BLUES?

WHY NOT SPEND SOME TIME IN YOUR
   MIND GARDEN?

- MOW YOUR MIND LAWN
- FERTILISE YOUR MIND MARROW
- TRIM YOUR MIND BUSH

AND IF IT ALL GETS TOO MUCH
YOU CAN ALWAYS TAKE YOURSELF
OFF TO YOUR MIND SHED.

# WELLNESS CLINIC

ARE YOU SUFFERING FROM AN ACUTE STRESS
REACTION, FOLLOWING THE RESULT OF
THE REFERENDUM?

WATCH OUT FOR THE FOLLOWING SYMPTOMS:
- CLAMMY HANDS
- DIZZINESS
- LOWER THAN NORMAL HEART RATE
- LOWER THAN NORMAL EXCHANGE RATE
- INCREASED LEVELS OF UNEMPLOYMENT
- INTENSE FEELINGS OF PANIC, ISOLATION
      AND DEPRESSION

IF YOU NOTICE ANY OF THESE SYMPTOMS,
 YOU SHOULD VISIT A DOCTOR IMMEDIATELY.
OR WHY NOT COLOUR IN ANOTHER PICTURE?

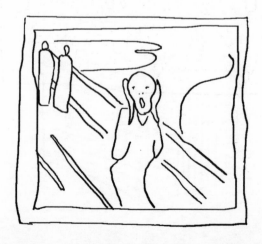

# ANGER CHUNNEL

IGNITE YOUR EMOTIONS & RATIONALISE YOUR FEELINGS. HOW DOES THIS IMAGE MAKE YOU FEEL?

# STERLING EMULATION

WITH USED TOILET ROLLS & STICKY TAPE
FASHION A CHUTE THROUGH WHICH YOU
CAN ROLL £1 COINS.

ATTACH THE END OF THE CHUTE TO
THE TOILET & ROLL AWAY.

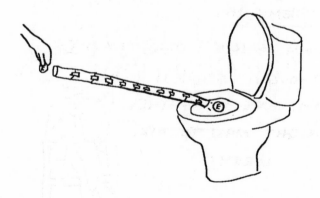

# ASK JEREMY

## SELF - IMAGE

"DEAR JEREMY — I CAN'T HELP ACTING LIKE A BUFFOON IN PUBLIC. IF IT'S NOT GETTING STUCK ON A ZIPWIRE, OR CRUSHING CHINESE SCHOOLCHILDREN THEN IT'S GETTING BEHIND A FOOLISH AND ULTIMATELY DESTRUCTIVE CAMPAIGN TO RUIN EVERYTHING. WHAT SHOULD I DO?"

BORIS (UXBRIDGE)

## JEREMY SAYS:

HMM... TOUGH ONE! HAVING THOUGHT ABOUT IT I AM NOT SURE I AM THE RIGHT MAN TO ASK. SORRY!

# WEALTH AND FITNESS

THE GB OLYMPIC TEAM IN 2016
BROUGHT BACK ENOUGH GOLD TO
BUOY UP OUR FAILING ECONOMY.
HOW MUCH GOLD CAN YOU WIN
BY EXERCISING DAILY?

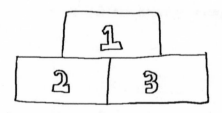

10 PRESS-UPS = 1 MEDAL

10K RUN = 10 MEDALS

5 SQUATS = 1 MEDAL

A WALK IN THE PARK = 1 MEDAL

# BRAIN SPRINT

## WHERE'S GEORGE HIDING?

ANSWER: ACTUALLY HE'S NOT HIDING AT ALL,
HE'S RIPPING IT UP ON HIS SPEEDBOAT IN
ST TROPEZ WITH ALL HIS CHUMS.

# FORGET THE BOX,

## THINK OUTSIDE THE UNION

WRITE YOUR IDEAS FOR POSSIBLE
TRADE PARTNERS HERE:

# BREXIT BREAKFAST

BEGIN YOUR DAY THE RIGHT WAY!
IMAGINE THE PERFECT CONTINENTAL
BREAKFAST AND DRAW IT ON THE
PLATE BELOW:

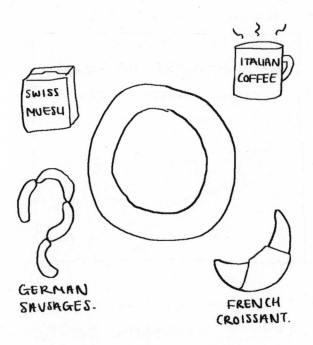

SWISS MUESU

ITALIAN COFFEE

GERMAN SAVSAGES.

FRENCH CROISSANT.

ALTERNATIVELY RISK A CORONARY WITH
A FULL ENGLISH.

# BROADEN YOUR HORIZONS

LEARN A NEW LANGUAGE!

TRANSLATE THIS GERMAN SENTENCE:

ICH SCHÄME MICH FÜR MEINE LANDS
ANSICHTEN ÜBER EINWANDERUNG UND
ES IST WIRKLICH BEMERKENSWERT,
WIE SIE IHRE ZÜGE PUNKTLICH.*

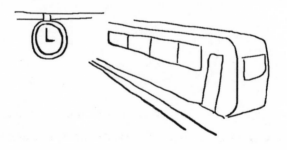

* I AM ASHAMED OF MY COMPATRIOTS'
  VIEWS ON IMMIGRATION AND IT IS
  TRULY REMARKABLE HOW YOUR
  TRAINS RUN ON TIME.

# POST REFERENDUM PAPERCRAFT

## THERAPY

USE THE BLANK SPACE UNDERNEATH TO DRAW SOME
THINGS YOU'RE LOOKING FORWARD TO →
   YOUR CHILDREN GROWING UP HAPPILY
FOR EXAMPLE, OR A COMFORTABLE RETIREMENT.

NEXT, TEAR OUT THIS PAGE ALONG THE DOTTED LINE.
CAREFULLY FOLD IT INTO THE SHAPE OF A CRUMPLED
PIECE OF PAPER AND PUT IT IN THE BIN.

NOW YOU NO LONGER HAVE TO BLAME 17,40,742
OTHER PEOPLE FOR THROWING AWAY YOUR FUTURE.

REMEMBER — TAKING RESPONSIBILITY FOR THINGS
   GIVES US STRENGTH.

# MAKE TIME FOR YOURSELF

SET YOUR WATCH AN HOUR AHEAD — THAT WAY YOU'LL ALWAYS BE IN SYNC WITH THE REST OF EUROPE AND HOPELESSLY OUT OF STEP WITH YOUR FELLOW COUNTRYMEN AND WOMEN.

# CORBYN CRAFT CORNER:

## CROCHET

CROCHET A COLOURFUL BLANKET
AND DRAPE IT OVER YOURSELF.

NOW WHEN PEOPLE ASK YOUR
OPINION, YOU CAN PRETEND
TO BE ASLEEP.

# EMBRACE CHANGE POST

## REFERENDUM

ALTERNATIVES TO EUROPEAN STYLE:

PORSCHE 911 $\longrightarrow$ FORD FOCUS

PRADA $\longrightarrow$ DOROTHY PERKINS

THE EIFFEL TOWER $\longrightarrow$ THE BLACKPOOL TOWER

THIERRY HENRY $\longrightarrow$ ERIC BRISTOW

# MOUSTACHE THERAPY

BELOW IS A SELECTION OF EUROPEAN
MOUSTACHES FOR YOU TO CUT OUT AND
WEAR WHEN YOU'RE FEELING BAD:

'THE BAVARIAN
FOAM GUARD'

'THE DÉTECTIVE
BELGE'

'THE GREEK
LEGEND'

'THE SPANISH
FLY'

# IMAGINARIUM

IMAGINE YOU'RE A POLITICIAN AND
MAKE UP SOME AMAZING STORIES.

HERE ARE SOME TITLES TO
GET YOU STARTED:

### 1. INVASION OF THE EVIL IMMIGRANTS

### 2. "WE'RE GONNA BE RICH!!"

### 3. "LET'S GIVE OUR NHS THE £350 MILLION THE EU TAKES EVERY WEEK."

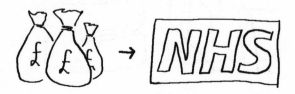

# EXPLORE YOUR JEALOUS EMOTIONS

IMAGINE THAT YOU ARE AT THE FRONT DOOR OF A BIG HOUSE.

INSIDE THERE IS A WONDERFUL BIRTHDAY PARTY TAKING PLACE.

THEY'VE GOT MUSIC & GAMES & DELICIOUS CAKE.

EVERYONE IS INVITED....

EXCEPT YOU, BECAUSE YOU VOTED TO LEAVE THE PARTY, DIDN'T YOU?

SILLY BILLY.

# FORGIVENESS ALLOTMENT

IN YOUR GARDEN, PLANT A TOMATO SEED
FOR EVERYONE YOU KNOW WHO VOTED 'LEAVE'.
OVER TIME, THE SEEDS WILL GROW
INTO PLANTS AND BEAR DELICIOUS FRUIT.

SEE HOW SOMETHING POSITIVE CAN COME
FROM SOMETHING BAD?

PLUS, NOW YOU'VE GOT SOMETHING TO PELT YOUR
BREXIT-VOTING FRIENDS AND FAMILY WITH NEXT
TIME THEY TRY TO VISIT.

# POSITIVE SPIN

N ATIONAL TREASURE

I NTEGRATOR

G LAMOROUS

E ASY-GOING

L OVING

# ESCAPISM

IF YOU'RE REALLY WORRIED ABOUT BEING
TRAPPED IN THE UK, YOU COULD CONSIDER
DIGGING AN ESCAPE TUNNEL FROM BRITAIN
TO MAINLAND EUROPE.

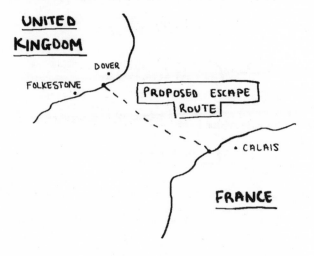

ASSUMING YOU CAN MUSTER A WORKFORCE
OF AROUND 15,000 PEOPLE, IT SHOULD
ONLY TAKE YOU AROUND 6 YEARS AND
COST APPROXIMATELY £12 BILLION
    TO COMPLETE.

# REWARD STATION

DID YOU FIND YOURSELF
PRETENDING THAT THE
REFERENDUM NEVER HAPPENED
TODAY?

IF NOT THEN WELL DONE.
REWARD YOURSELF WITH A
SOOTHING MUG OF BOVRIL.

# POSITIVITY CHECK

REASONS TO BE CHEERFUL:

- CROWN GREEN BOWLS

- ICELAND (NOT THE COUNTRY)

- CORBY TROUSER PRESS

- GOOD IRRIGATION

- IAN BOTHAM

- SHOWADDYWADDY

- FISHERMAN'S FRIEND

- TANK TOPS

- UMBRO SPORTS CLOTHING

- JILLY COOPER

# POSITIVITY CHECK

SEE IF YOU CAN THINK OF ANY
MORE REASONS TO BE CHEERFUL

- 
- 
- 
- 
- 
-

# THE CONFIDENCE CHAIR

SIT DOWN. DRAW FROM
YOUR CONFIDENCE WELL.

YOU ARE ENTITLED,

YOU ARE A CHAMPION,

YOU ARE FULFILLING YOUR DESTINY,

YOU ARE SUPERIOR.

NOW YOU KNOW HOW BORIS

FEELS EVERYDAY.

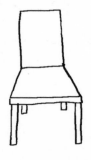

# SILVER LININGS

AT LEAST OUR EXIT FROM THE EU
MUST SURELY MEAN AN EXIT FROM
COMPETING IN THE EUROVISION SONG CONTEST?

WAIT — AUSTRALIA ARE NOW
ELIGIBLE FOR ENTRY?

# LEARN TO BE

# STRONGER ALONE

# TACKLING THE FIVE
## STAGES OF GRIEF

### 5. ACCEPTANCE

LEARN TO LIVE IN THIS, THE NEW
REALITY OF POST REFERENDUM NOWNESS.

1) TAKE AN OBJECT LIKE A
   PORK PIE OR A COPY OF THE SUN.

2) TRACE YOUR FINGER AROUND
   ITS EDGES, EXPLORE ITS AROMA.
   CAREFULLY CARESS ITS TEXTURE.

NOW THAT WASN'T SO DIFFICULT,
WAS IT?

# SEE THINGS FROM THE OTHER SIDE

CUT OUT THE GLASSES BELOW AND
FIT THEM WITH ROSE-TINTED LENSES.

LOOK BACK AT THE PRE-EU BRITAIN
OF THE 1970s. THE GLASSES WILL FILTER
OUT THE UNEMPLOYMENT, INFLATION, PICKET
LINES, RACIAL TENSION, SIDEBURNS
AND SO ON...

NOW PRETEND THAT BY LEAVING THE EU,
BRITAIN WILL SOMEHOW BE RESTORED TO AN
IMAGINARY FORMER GLORY - FREE FROM ANY
UNEMPLOYMENT, INFLATION, PICKET LINES,
RACIAL TENSIONS OR SIDEBURNS.

YOU CAN NOW EITHER REMOVE THE GLASSES
AND RETURN TO REALITY, OR KEEP
THEM AND JOIN UKIP.

# BREXIT PETTING ZOO

LEARN TO LOVE YOUR ADVERSARY.
PERSONALISE THEM.

PET YOUR
MICHAEL GOVE
GERBIL.

# UNLEASH YOUR INNER COIFFEUR

HELP NIGEL DISGUISE HIMSELF
AND DRAW ON A MANLY
MOUSTACHE.

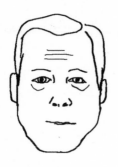

MAYBE IT WILL HELP HIM GET
THROUGH CUSTOMS WHEN HE
HOLIDAYS IN EUROPE.

# CONCENTRATION HOOPS

IMMERSE YOURSELF IN UNACHIEVABLE
GOALS TO ALLEVIATE ANXIETY.

WHY NOT TAKE A NEEDLE AND SOME
SEWING SCISSORS & TRY TO UNPICK
40 YEARS OF UK LAW FROM 40
YEARS OF EU LAW.

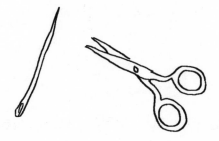

# POST-REFERENDUM PAPERCRAFT

## <u>THERAPY</u>

IF YOU'RE FEELING HOMESICK FOR THE EU,
TRY THIS:

- PHOTOCOPY THIS PAGE.

- NOW PHOTOCOPY IT AGAIN 16,000 TIMES.

- TIE ALL THE SHEETS OF PAPER UP IN RED
TAPE AND CHARGE YOURSELF £12.5 BILLION
A YEAR TO UNTIE IT ALL AGAIN.

FEELING MORE AT HOME NOW?

# PULSE RESPONSE

PUT YOUR FINGERS ON THE PULSE
POINTS ON YOUR NECK. CHECK
THAT YOU HAVE A STEADY RHYTHM.

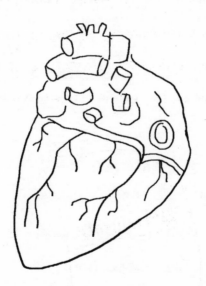

NOW TURN THE PAGE
→

# WE'RE LEAVING
## THE EU!!

KEEP MEASURING YOUR PULSE.

DID THE RATE INCREASE?

YES: WE STILL HAVE WORK TO DO.

NO: WELL DONE.

# HAPPY ENDING?

YOU SHOULD NOW HAVE COMPLETED
YOUR JOURNEY OF ACCEPTANCE.

YOU ARE READY TO
CLOSE THE BOOK ON THIS
CHAPTER OF YOUR LIFE.

... AND NOW IT'S TIME TO LITERALLY CLOSE THIS BOOK.

... NO REALLY ...
IT'S FINISHED ...

CLOSE THE
BLOODY BOOK!